SO-AFX-140

A Curious George® Activity Book

I Am Curious About the Four Seasons

Featuring
Margret and H.A. Rey's
Curious George

SCHOLASTIC INC.

New York Toronto London Auckland Sydney

Activities by Jan Carr
Illustrations by Manny Campana

No part of this publication may be reproduced in whole or in part,
or stored in a retrieval system, or transmitted in any form or by any means,
electronic, mechanical, photocopying, recording, or otherwise,
without written permission of the publisher.
For information regarding permission, write to Houghton Mifflin Company,
2 Park Street, Boston, MA 02108.

ISBN 0-590-41873-4

Copyright © 1984 by Houghton Mifflin Company and Curgeo Agencies, Inc.
Copyright © 1988 by Scholastic Books, Inc.
Curious George ® is a registered trademark of Margret Rey.
This publication is based on the Houghton Mifflin book series adapted from the Curious Geroge film series,
edited by Margret Rey and Alan J. Shalleck,
published with the permission of Houghton Mifflin Company.
All rights reserved.   Published by Scholastic Inc.
730 Broadway, New York, NY 10003, by arrangement with Houghton Mifflin Company.

12 11 10 9 8 7 6 5 4 3 2 1   8 9/8 0 1 2 3/9

Printed in the U.S.A.   34
First Scholastic Printing, November 1988

This is George.
He lives with the man
with the yellow hat.

George is very curious.
He is curious about you.
Write your name here.

MARTElena Mantería

George is also very curious
about the seasons.
When is your birthday?
Circle the season in which
you were born.

(WINTER) (SPRING) SUMMER FALL

If you are curious about
the answers to the puzzles,
look in the back of the book.

WINTER

It was a cold, frosty winter morning.
"It snowed last night, George,"
said the man with the yellow hat.
"Let's try our new sled."
In each row, circle the snowflakes that are alike.

George and the man with the yellow hat went to the hill.
Put an X through the people on the hill who are not doing winter activities.

The Ramirez family was making a snowman.
Circle the clothes they need to wear in winter.

George wanted to make a snowman, too.
He started to roll a snowball.
The first snowman is already finished.
You can finish the rest.

The snowball got bigger and bigger until it was so big George couldn't see over it. In each line, circle the thing that is the biggest.

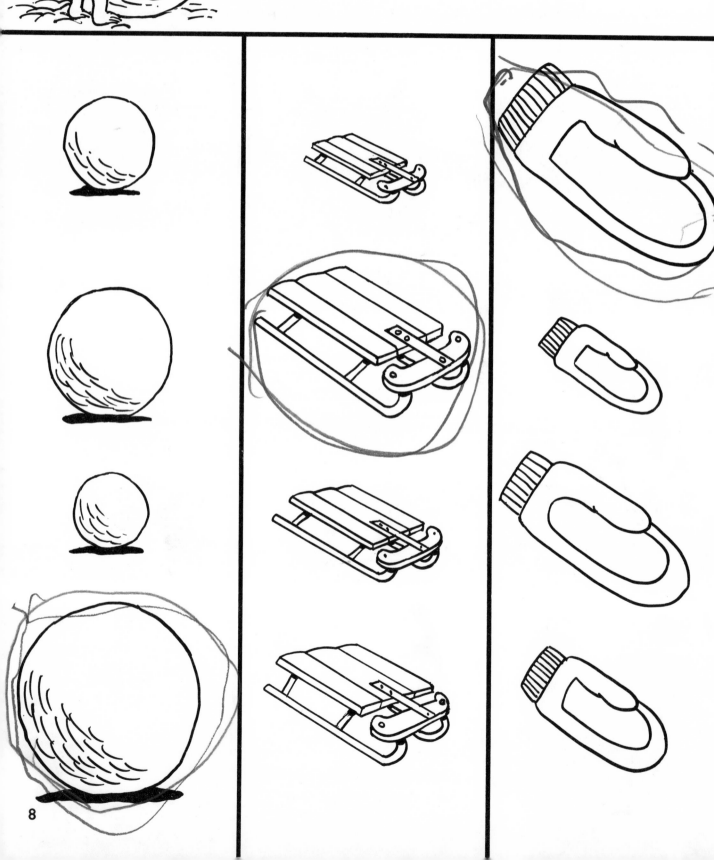

8

"Here comes an avalanche!" someone cried.
The snowball rolled down the hill
and knocked over some skiers.
These skiers are skiing down a hill.
Draw a square around the one who has skied the farthest.
Draw a triangle around the one who is dressed most warmly.
Draw a circle around the one who is the tallest.

At the top of the hill, Jimmy Ramirez
climbed on a sled.
He was too little to sled by himself.
"Watch out, Jimmy!" shouted his mother.
These children need help in the snow.
Draw a line from each child to the thing
he or she needs.

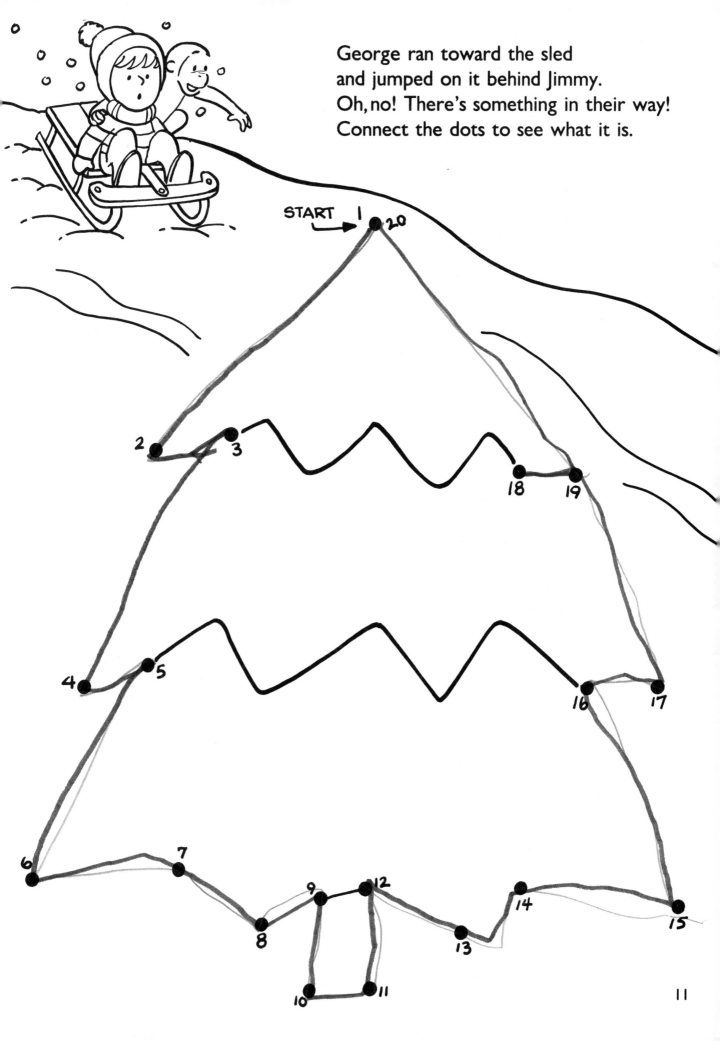

George ran toward the sled
and jumped on it behind Jimmy.
Oh, no! There's something in their way!
Connect the dots to see what it is.

START

11

George held on to Jimmy and steered the sled safely down the hill.
Help George find the right path.

START

FINISH

12

"George saved Jimmy!" shouted Mrs. Ramirez.
"Three cheers for George!"
Color in all the pictures below
that you saw in this story.

SPRING

It was a warm, sunny spring day.
George was going for a hike with his friends
Suzie and Ted.
What was George doing before they left?
Connect the dots and see.

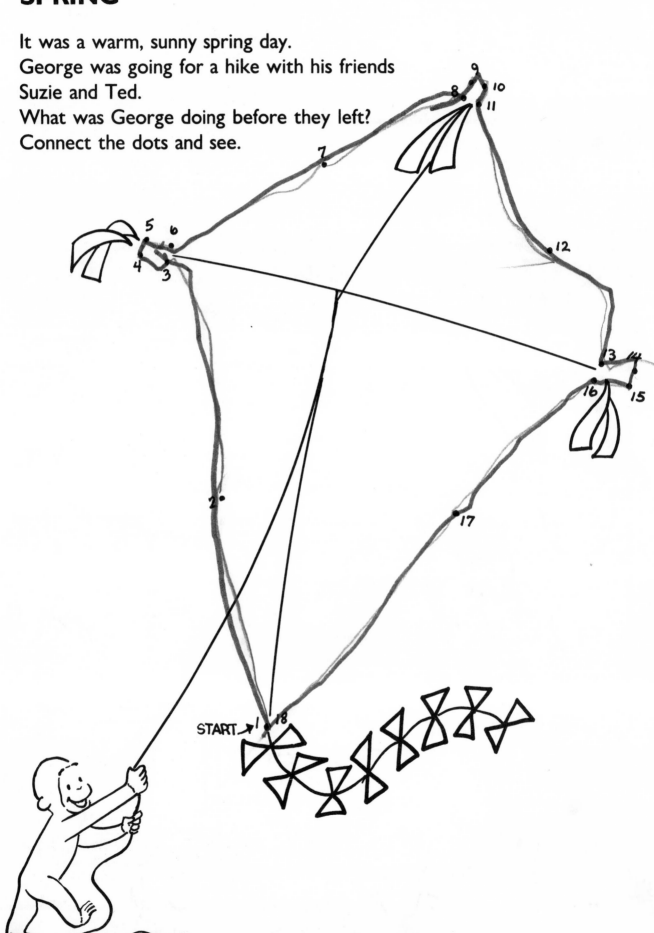

"George, you carry this bag of marshmallows," said Suzie.
They started down the trail.
The trail was dotted with flowers.
Color the Number 1 flowers pink,
the Number 2 flowers red, and the
Number 3 flowers yellow.

"Look! There's a cardinal!" whispered Ted.
George, Suzie, and Ted saw lots of birds that day.
Some of the birds' names are scrambled here.
Unscramble them in the spaces below.
The numbers will tell you how.

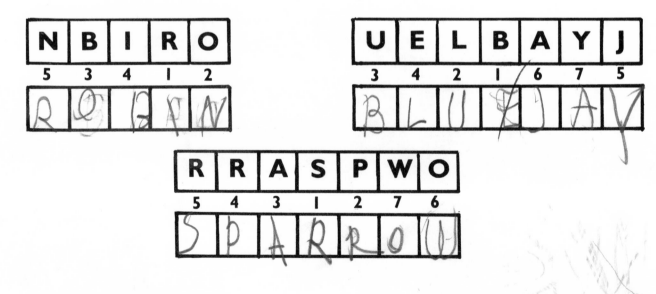

N	B	I	R	O
5	3	4	1	2

R O B I N

U	E	L	B	A	Y	J
3	4	2	1	6	7	5

B L U E J A Y

R	R	A	S	P	W	O
5	4	3	1	2	7	6

S P A R R O W

N	C	H	I	F
3	4	5	2	1

F I N C H

L	E	R	B	W	R	A
5	6	7	4	1	3	2

W A R B L E R

George tripped and dropped the bag of marshmallows. It hit a sharp rock and split wide open. Some of the things on this page are sharp and hard. Others are very soft. Draw a line from each picture to the word that describes it.

hard   soft

hard   soft

hard   soft

hard   soft

17

Not far down the trail they saw a deer.
"Look!" Ted called.
Lots of other animals also lived along the trail.
Find them in the picture and color them in.

George picked up the bag of marshmallows
and ran after the deer.
He did not notice the rip in the bag.
The marshmallows fell out,
one by one.
Add the marshmallows to find out how many fell out.

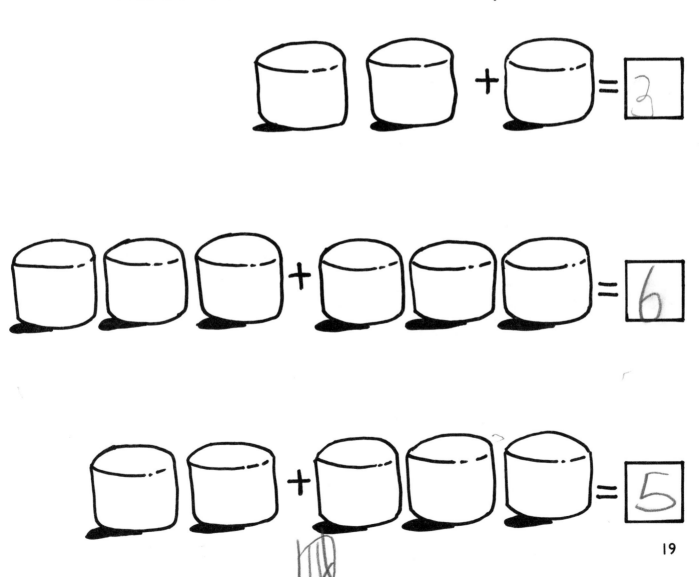

George and his friends chased the deer
across a little brook.
But the deer was too fast for them.
George stopped to count the tadpoles.
How many can you count?

3+3 =6

"I'm hungry," said Suzie.
"Let's eat the marshmallows now."
She stopped by a patch of wildflowers.
Solve the rebus to find out how they grow.

April Showers brings
May Flowers

George held up the bag.
Not a single marshmallow was left.
He started to cry.
"We'd better take you home," said Suzie.
The names of eight spring flowers
are hidden in the word search puzzle below.
Circle the ones you find.

WORD LIST

crocus   violet

daisy   lilac

daffodil   lily

tulip   jonquil

D A I S Y V Q C

A J T U L I P R

F O K D E O S O

F N S L I L A C

O Q G H N E T U

D U V W X T L S

I I Y Z J A P B

L L I L Y J R A

"We're lost!" said Ted.
"How do we get home?"
Help them find the way.
Some of the paths lead farther
into the woods.
Only one path leads home.

START

CAVE

WOODS

BEAR

POND

HOME

FINISH

George knew what to do.
He took Ted and Suzie by the hand.
They followed the trail of spilled
marshmallows right back
to where they came from.
Take your pencil and trace the shape
the marshmallows make.
Where did Suzie, Ted, and George end up?

START →

SUMMER

It was a sunny, hot summer day.
"Let's go fishing, George,"
said the man with the yellow hat.
They took their fishing poles
and drove to the country.
S is for summer. Color all the
summer things that begin with **S** in this picture.

SUN TAN OIL

"This looks like a good place," said the man.
"I'll look for a shallow spot."
These things are in the picture below.
Color them in when you find them.

George decided to swing through the trees. Each tree has its own special kind of leaf.

Draw a line from each leaf to the branch it belongs to.

He saw a family that was camping in the woods.
What things did they need for their trip?
Match the pictures with the words in the word list.
Then write the words in the numbered squares.

WORD LIST
canteen
tent
canoe
knapsack

DOWN

1.

ACROSS

2.

3.

4.

2. C A N O O

1. C
A
N
T
3. T E N T
E
E

4. K N A P S A C K

They were getting ready for a picnic.
Who else wants to come to the picnic?
To find out, print the names of the pictures below,
and then copy down the letters in the boxes.

WAVE

SUN

TREE

NEST

ANTS

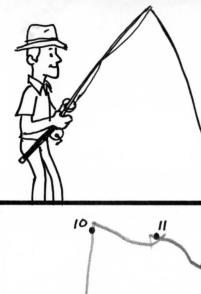

The father was fishing.
His basket was full of fish.
Connect the dots to see how many.

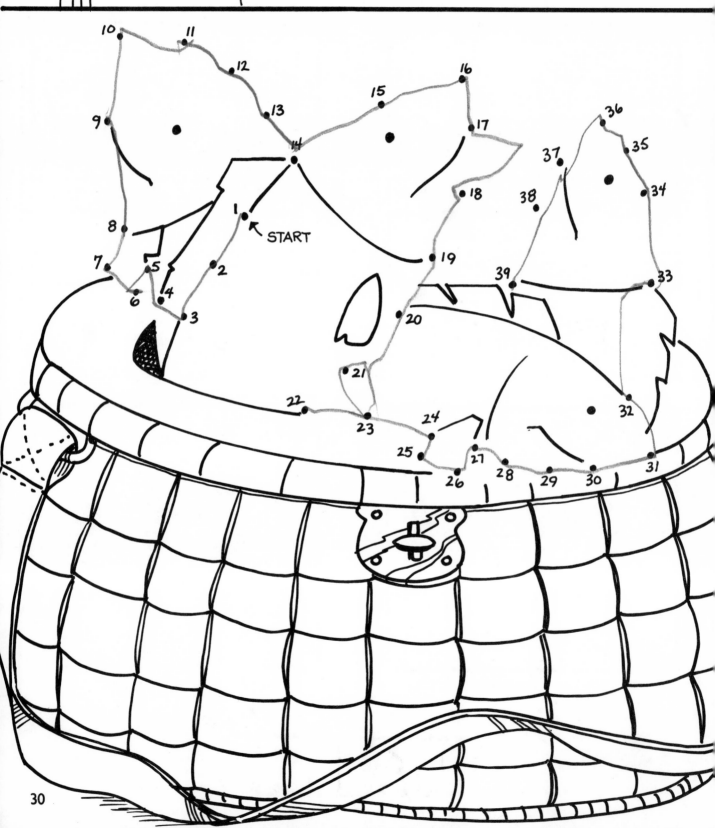

START

30

George was curious.
He climbed down from the tree.
How does George get down the tree?
Color the correct picture.

George found the family's fishing poles.
He picked up all four.
What's under the water near George?
Color the things that belong there,
and cross out the ones that don't.

"He got a bite!" the little girl said.
She was setting out lots of summer fruits
for the picnic. Unscramble the words
to see what they were.
The numbers below will help you.

R	R	E	H	C	I	E	S
5	4	3	2	1	6	7	8

CHERRIES

C	H	S	E	A	E	P
4	5	7	2	3	6	1

PEACHES

U	E	B	L	R	R	B	E	S	I	E
3	4	1	2	8	7	5	6	11	9	10

BLUEBERRIES

L	P	S	M	U
2	1	5	4	3

PLUMS

T	E	R	W	A	O	N	M	E	L
3	4	5	1	2	9	10	6	7	8

WATERMELON

33

George tugged and tugged.
He caught four fat shiny fish.
There are more fish hidden in this picture.
Circle them when you find them.

The family cooked the fish and ate them for lunch.
They were delicious.
Especially for George, the fisherman.
Can you remember what happened in the story?
Put the pictures in the right order.

FALL

It was a cool, crisp fall afternoon.
George and the man with the yellow hat
were carving a jack-o-lantern.
You can make a jack-o-lantern, too.
Pick the eyes, nose, and mouth you like best
and draw them in.

The phone rang.
It was Aunt Harriet.
She invited them to her party.
Aunt Harriet was busy decorating her house.
Unscramble the words to find out what she was using.
The numbers below will help you.

C	S	A	E	R	W	O	R	C
2	1	3	5	4	9	8	7	6

K	N	S	I	U	M	P	P
5	7	8	6	2	3	1	4

O	U	R	S	D	G
2	3	4	6	5	1

Y	A	H	S	C	T	A	K	S
3	2	1	4	7	5	6	8	9

N	I	N	I	A	D	R	O	C	N
6	1	2	4	5	3	9	8	7	10

37

"Come on, George," said his friend.
"Let's go."
On the way, they saw many trees turning colors.
Color the leaves on the Number 1 trees red,
the leaves on the Number 2 trees yellow,
and the leaves on the Number 3 trees orange.

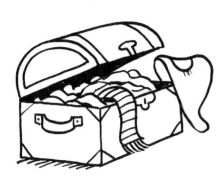

"Where is your costume?" said Aunt Harriet.
"This is a Halloween party.
  Why don't you go up to the attic
  and make your own costume?
  There are lots of old clothes there."
What would *you* like to be for Halloween?
Draw a picture of yourself in your favorite costume.

In the attic, George found a fireman's hat.
It was too big.
There were lots of other hats in the attic, too.
Draw a line from each hat to the person who needs it.

40

On top of an old dresser was a big white sheet.
George was curious.
Could he use that?
What do you think George will be?
Connect the dots to find out.

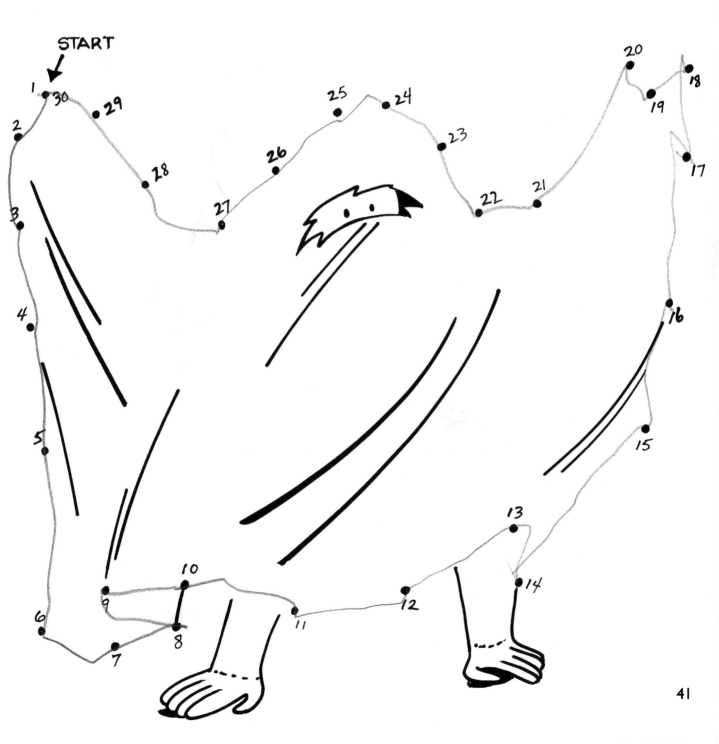

START

George became tangled in the sheet.
He got scared and
ran down the stairs.
The two pictures below are almost the same, but not quite.
In the second picture there are some things missing.
Circle the places where they should be.

 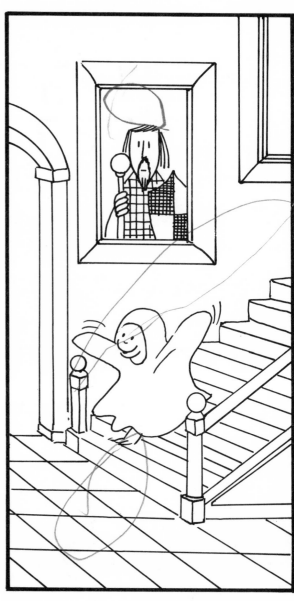

BOO-o.o.o.o

All the guests had arrived.
"Look!" someone shouted.
"There goes a ghost!"
What were the guests dressed as?
Fill in the crossword puzzle to find out.

WORD LIST

ballerina
gypsy
soldier
cowboy
princess

DOWN

1.
2.

ACROSS

3.
4.
5.

George tripped on the rug and flew through the air.
"Aahh!" screamed the guests, but George felt fine.
He liked to fly.
He was soaring like a bird.
Outside, these birds were flying south for the winter.
Circle the bird who does not belong.

"George!" said Aunt Harriet.
"It's you! You certainly gave us a scare
dressed as a ghost!"
There are many ghosts hidden in this picture.
Circle the ones you find.

"He should win the costume contest!"
someone shouted.
They pinned a big ribbon on George's costume.
It said, "First prize."
Do you remember which season is which?
Write the name of the season
underneath each picture.

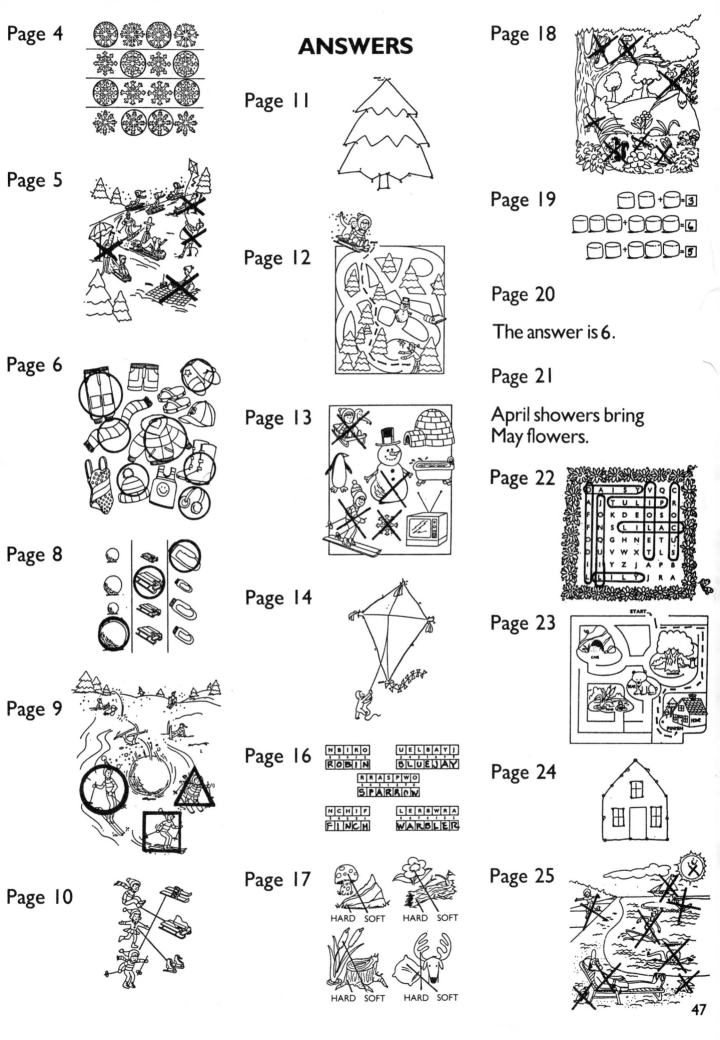

ANSWERS

Page 4

Page 5

Page 6

Page 8

Page 9

Page 10

Page 11

Page 12

Page 13

Page 14

Page 16

NBIRO
ROBIN

UELBAYJ
BLUEJAY

RRASPWO
SPARROW

NCHIF
FINCH

LERBWRA
WARBLER

Page 17

HARD SOFT   HARD SOFT

HARD SOFT   HARD SOFT

Page 18

Page 19

$$\square\square + \square = 3$$
$$\square\square\square + \square\square\square = 6$$
$$\square\square + \square\square\square = 5$$

Page 20

The answer is 6.

Page 21

April showers bring
May flowers.

Page 22

Page 23

Page 24

Page 25

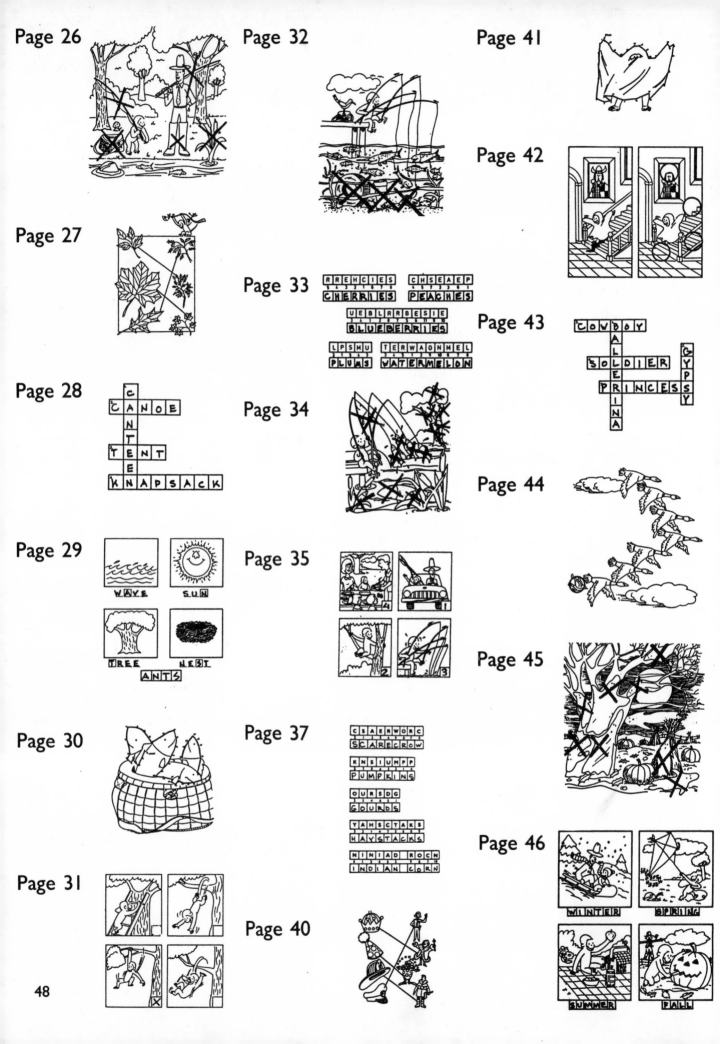

Page 26

Page 27

Page 28

Page 29

Page 30

Page 31

Page 32

Page 33

CHERRIES PEACHES

BLUEBERRIES

PLUMS WATERMELON

Page 34

Page 35

Page 37

SCARECROW

PUMPKINS

GOURDS

HAYSTACKS

INDIAN CORN

Page 40

Page 41

Page 42

Page 43

Page 44

Page 45

Page 46

48